Put Beginning Readers on the Right Track with
ALL ABOARD READING™

The All Aboard Reading series is especially designed for beginning readers. Written by noted authors and illustrated in full color, these are books that children really want to read—books to excite their imagination, expand their interests, make them laugh, and support their feelings. With fiction and nonfiction stories that are high interest and curriculum-related, All Aboard Reading books offer something for every young reader. And with four different reading levels, the All Aboard Reading series lets you choose which books are most appropriate for your children and their growing abilities.

Picture Readers
Picture Readers have super-simple texts, with many nouns appearing as rebus pictures. At the end of each book are 24 flash cards—on one side is a rebus picture; on the other side is the written-out word.

Station Stop 1
Station Stop 1 books are best for children who have just begun to read. Simple words and big type make these early reading experiences more comfortable. Picture clues help children to figure out the words on the page. Lots of repetition throughout the text helps children to predict the next word or phrase—an essential step in developing word recognition.

Station Stop 2
Station Stop 2 books are written specifically for children who are reading with help. Short sentences make it easier for early readers to understand what they are reading. Simple plots and simple dialogue help children with reading comprehension.

Station Stop 3
Station Stop 3 books are perfect for children who are reading alone. With longer text and harder words, these books appeal to children who have mastered basic reading skills. More complex stories captivate children who are ready for more challenging books.

In addition to All Aboard Reading books, look for All Aboard Math Readers™ (fiction stories that teach math concepts children are learning in school) and All Aboard Science Readers™ (nonfiction books that explore the most fascinating science topics in age-appropriate language).

All Aboard for happy reading!

To all of my family and friends, with love—T.P.

Text copyright © 2003 by Tracey West. Illustrations copyright © 2003 by Tamara Petrosino.
All rights reserved. Published by Grosset & Dunlap, a division of Penguin Putnam Books for
Young Readers, 345 Hudson Street, New York, NY 10014. GROSSET & DUNLAP and ALL
ABOARD MATH READER are trademarks of Penguin Putnam Inc. Published simultaneously
in Canada. Printed in the U.S.A.

Library of Congress Cataloging-in-Publication Data is available.

ISBN 0-448-43112-2 (pbk)   A   B   C   D   E   F   G   H   I   J
ISBN 0-448-43138-6 (GB)   A   B   C   D   E   F   G   H   I   J

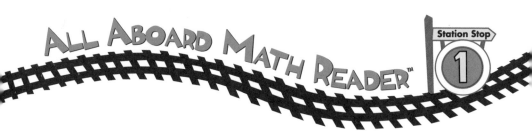

By Jayne Harvey
Illustrated by Tamara Petrosino

Grosset & Dunlap • New York

It is time for the cat show.

The kids must get the cats
ready for the show.

Their parents will be here soon.
How will the kids group the cats?

7

Pam thinks of a way
to sort the cats.

Some cats are big.

Some cats are small.

The cats are in groups.

There are seven big cats.

There are three small cats.

Oh, no!
Some of the small cats
want to play.

Matt thinks of another way
to sort the cats.

Some cats
have stripes.

Some cats
have no stripes.

The cats are in groups.

There are four cats
with stripes.

14

There are six cats
without stripes.

15

Oh, no!
Some of the striped cats
want to fight!

Jake thinks of another way
to sort the cats.

Some cats have
blue eyes.

Some cats have
green eyes.

The cats are in groups.

There are five cats
with green eyes.

There are five cats
with blue eyes.

Oh, no!
Some of the cats
with green eyes
want to run around.

Will thinks of another way
to sort the cats.

Some cats have gray fur.
Some cats have orange fur.
Some cats have black fur.
Some cats have white fur.

The cats are in groups.

There are four cats
with gray fur.

There are three cats
with orange fur.

There are two cats
with black fur.
There is one cat
with white fur.

Oh, no!
Some of the gray cats
want to make noise.

Kim thinks of another way
to sort the cats.
One cat has a hat.
Some cats have no hats.

The cats are in groups.

There is one cat with a hat.

There are nine cats with no hats.

There is one mouse.

One mouse?

The cats chase the mouse.

The kids chase the cats.

The cats are tired.
Now the cats are
in one big group.

All ten cats are asleep.

The sleeping cats are so cute.

The parents are very proud.

The cat show is a hit!